The
Great Big
Book of
Bedtime
Stories
and Rhyme

NEW
BURLINGTON
BOOKS

A NEW BURLINGTON BOOK
The Old Brewery
6 Blundell Street
London N7 9BH

Conceived, edited and designed by
QED Publishing
A Quarto Group Company
226 City Road
London EC1V 2TT
www.qed-publishing.co.uk

ISBN 978-1-84538-882-9

Publisher: Steve Evans
Creative Director: Zeta Davies
Senior Editor: Hannah Ray

Printed and bound in China

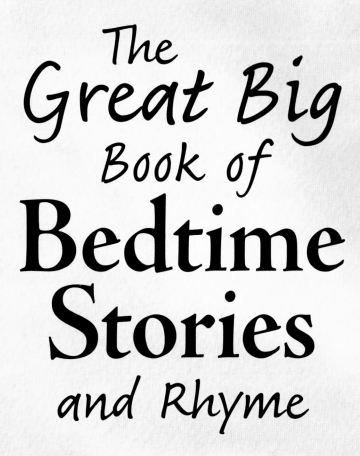

The
Great Big
Book of
Bedtime
Stories
and Rhyme

Contents

When I'm a Grownup

Anne Faundez

Illustrated by Katherine Lucas

When I'm a grownup,
Who will I be?

10

A bird in the air,

Or a fish in the sea?

When I'm a grownup,
What will I do?

Fly a spaceship to Mars,
Or work in a zoo?

13

When I'm a grownup,
Will I be tall?

Huge like a hippo,

Or round like a ball?

When I'm a grownup, what will I eat?

Pineapple pie, or some other treat?

When I'm a grownup,

Who will live with me?

A frog or a dog?

Or a hoppity flea?

When I'm a grownup, what will I wear?

Hmm, let me see, I really don't care!

When I'm a grownup,
Will I travel by car?

Ride on a rhino,

Or swing from a star?

When I'm a grownup,
I really don't mind
Who I will be...

As long as

I'm

ME!

Sing a Song of Sixpence

Compiled by Anne Faundez
Illustrated by Simone Abel

Sing a Song of Sixpence

Sing a song of sixpence,
A pocket full of rye,
Four and twenty blackbirds
Baked in a pie.

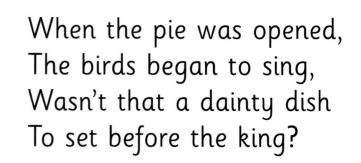

When the pie was opened,
The birds began to sing,
Wasn't that a dainty dish
To set before the king?

The king was in his counting house,
Counting out his money,
The queen was in the parlor,
Eating bread and honey.

The maid was in the garden,
Hanging out the clothes,
There came a little blackbird
And snapped off her nose.

Little Jack Horner

Little Jack Horner sat in a corner
Eating his Christmas pie,
He put in his thumb and pulled out a plum,
And said what a good boy am I!

Little Miss Muffet

Little Miss Muffet
Sat on a tuffet,
Eating her curds and whey.
Along came a spider
Who sat down beside her,
And frightened Miss Muffet away.

Here We Go 'Round the Mulberry Bush

Here we go 'round
   the mulberry bush,
The mulberry bush,
   the mulberry bush,
Here we go 'round
   the mulberry bush,
On a cold and
   frosty morning.

This is the way we
   wash our hands,
Wash our hands,
   wash our hands,
This is the way we
   wash our hands,
On a cold and
   frosty morning.

This is the way we
   brush our teeth,
Brush our teeth,
   brush our teeth,
This is the way we
   brush our teeth,
On a cold and
   frosty morning.

This is the way we
   go to school,
Go to school,
   go to school,
This is the way we
   go to school,
On a cold and
   frosty morning.

One, Two, Three, Four, Five

One, two, three, four, five,
Once I caught a fish alive.
Six, seven, eight, nine, ten,
Then I let it go again.

Why did you let it go?
Because it bit my finger so.
Which finger did it bite?
This little finger on the right.

Two Little Dicky Birds

Two little dicky birds
Sitting on a wall,
One named Peter,
One named Paul.

Fly away, Peter!
Fly away, Paul!
Come back, Peter!
Come back, Paul!

Old King Cole

Old King Cole
Was a merry old soul,
And a merry old soul was he.
He called for his pipe and
He called for his bowl,
And he called for his fiddlers three.

Cock a Doodle Doo!

Cock a doodle doo!
My dame has lost her shoe,
My master's lost his fiddling stick,
And doesn't know what to do.

39

Hush, Little Baby

Hush, little baby, don't say a word,
Mama's going to buy you a mocking-bird.

And if that mocking-bird don't sing,
Mama's going to buy you a diamond ring.

And if that diamond ring turns brass,
Mama's going to buy you a looking glass.

And if that looking glass gets broke,
Mama's going to buy you a billy goat.

And if that billy goat won't pull,
Mama's going to buy you a cart and bull.

And if that cart and bull turn over,
Mama's going to buy you a dog
named Rover.

And if that dog named
Rover won't bark,
Mama's going to buy you
a horse and cart.

And if that horse and cart fall down,
You'll still be the sweetest little baby
in town.

Girls and Boys Come Out to Play

Girls and boys come out to play,
The moon doth shine as bright as day,
Leave your supper and leave your sleep,
And join your playfellows in the street.
Come with a hoop, come with a call,
Come and be merry, or not at all,
Up the ladder and over the wall,
A penny loaf will serve us all.

Wee Willie Winkie

Wee Willie Winkie
Runs through the town,
Upstairs and downstairs
In his nightgown,
Rapping at the window,
Crying through the lock,
Are the children in their beds,
For it's now eight o'clock?

Hush-a-bye, Baby

Hush-a-bye, baby, on the tree top,
When the wind blows, the cradle will rock.
When the bough breaks, the cradle will fall,
And down will come baby, cradle, and all.

Sleep, Baby, Sleep

Sleep, baby, sleep!
Thy father watches the sheep,
Thy mother is shaking the dreamland tree,
And down falls a little dream on thee.
Sleep, baby, sleep!

The Great Big Friend Hunt

Hannah Ray

Illustrated by Jacqueline East

Henry was a puppy.
A very small, very scruffy puppy.

He lived on a farm with Cleo the cat. Cleo was sleepy.
She never wanted to play with Henry.
Henry got very bored playing by himself.

When Henry was bored,
bad things seemed to happen.

And most of these happened
to poor Cleo!

"Oh, Henry," she sighed. "What you need is a friend. That would stop you from being bored."

Henry thought this sounded great. There was just one problem —what was a friend?

Henry headed into the yard where the other animals lived. He stood up, straight and tall—as straight and as tall as a small, scruffy dog can. In a loud voice he said,
"I am going on a Friend Hunt.
A Great **BIG** Friend Hunt.
Will any of you help me?"

Doug Donkey raised his head.
  "Hee-haw! I'll help you, Henry,"
he said.

  "Me, too," snorted Peggy the pig.

  "And me!" mooed Clara the cow.

Henry was very happy with
all this help. But there was still one
problem—none of the other animals
knew what a friend was either!

Doug Donkey decided to ask his
daddy, who was very wise.

"A friend," said Doug's daddy,
"is someone to talk to."

Doug Donkey trotted off
right away to tell Henry.

"Oh, thank you!" said Henry. "I'm so glad
you told me! Now we've found that out,
let's keep looking for a friend."

But they couldn't find one, and Henry
was starting to feel really disappointed.

Peggy asked her sister Petunia, who was very smart, if she knew what a friend was.

"Of course I do," replied Petunia.
"A friend cheers you up when you are sad."

"There you go!' exclaimed Peggy. "Now we know even more about friends. I'm sure we'll find one soon. Chin up, Henry."

Henry felt much better.

But the animals still couldn't find a friend. Henry was beginning to worry that the day was almost over.

Clara's cousin, Courtney, had come to stay. She knew so much about so many things. When Clara asked her what a friend was, she answered, "A friend is always happy to help."

With this in mind, the animals hunted high and low—but it was no use. They still couldn't find a friend... and it was starting to get dark.

"Don't worry, Henry," said Clara. "We'll help you look again tomorrow. And the day after that!"

61

"Oh, Cleo," sniffed Henry when they returned home. "We've hunted all day. We know a friend is someone to talk to. We know a friend cheers you up when you are sad. And we know a friend is always happy to help. But we just couldn't find one."

Cleo rolled her eyes, but she couldn't help smiling as she said, "A friend is someone to talk to? A friend cheers you up when you are sad? A friend is always happy to help?

You silly, small, scruffy dog! You haven't just found one friend...

you've found lots!"

65

Said Mouse
to Mole

Clare Bevan
Illustrated by Sanja Rescek

Said Mouse to Mole,
"How do you do?"

Said Mole to Mouse,
"And how are you?"

Said Mouse, "I'm feeling sad and blue."

Said Mole, "I'm feeling gloomy, too."

69

Said Mouse, "I wish that I could fly,
Like Bee and Bird across the sky."

Said Mole, "But if you fly around,
I'll miss you when I'm underground."

Said Mole, "I wish
that I could run,
Like Squirrel in the
summer sun."

Said Mouse, "But if you play outside, I'll miss you when I have to hide."

Said Mouse, "I wish that I could float,
Like Beetle in his sailboat."

Said Mole, "But if you sail away,
Who will talk to me all day?"

Said Mole, "I wish that I could sing,
Like Blackbird with his glossy wing."

Said Mouse, "But if you sing and shout,
The Big Bad Cat will prowl about!"

Said Mouse, "I wish that I could shine,
Like sunbeams in the summertime."

Said Mole, "But if
you're shiny bright,
The Big Bad Cat will
prowl all night."

Said Mole, "I wish that I could be
Taller than the tallest tree."

Said Mouse, "But if you grow so tall,
Your little house will be too small."

Said Mouse, "I wish that I could change
To something beautiful and strange."

Said Mole, "But if you're strange and new,
Will you like me? Will I like you?"

Said Mouse to Mole, said Mole to Mouse,
"Don't leave your home. Don't leave your house.
Don't be a snail. Don't be a star...

I LIKE YOU JUST THE WAY YOU ARE!"

Pet the Cat

Wes Magee
Illustrated by Pauline Siewert

Pet the Cat

Pet the cat,
   pet the cat
and lift it from the floor.

Pet the cat,
   pet the cat
and shake hands with its paw.

Pet the cat,
   pet the cat
and scratch its head once more.

Pet the cat,
   pet the cat
—then **shoo** it through the door!

In My Yard

There's a cat in my yard
with a wasp on her toes.
    Shake it off,
     shake it off.
Look,
    there
        it
          goes! Buzzzzzzzzzzzzzzzzzz

There's a dog in my yard
with a bee on his nose.
    Shake it off,
     shake it off.
Look,
    there
        it
          goes! Buzzzzzzzzzzzzzzzz

Recess

Children creeping,
children peeping,
children leaping, leaping, leaping.

Children teasing,
children wheezing,
children sneezing, sneezing, sneezing.

Children calling,
children falling,
children bawling, bawling, bawling.

Children hopping,
Children flopping.

There's the bell!

Children,
    children,
        children
            stopping.

Climb the Mountain

Climb
the
mountain
high,
touch
the
clouds
and
see
the
sky.
Feel
the
wind
against
you
blow,
see
the
fields
far
far
below.

Animal Chat

Dogs growl,
Wolves howl.
Cows moo,
Doves coo.
Lions roar,
Crows caw.
Horses neigh,
Donkeys bray.
Monkeys shriek,
Mice squeak.
Parrots squawk
...and I talk.

My Dog's First Poem
(To be read in a dog's voice)

My barking drives them
    up the wall.
I chew the carpet
    in the hall.
I love to chase
    a bouncing...**banana**?

Everywhere I leave
    long hairs.
I fight the cushions
    on the chairs.
Just watch me race
    right up the...**shower**?

94

Once I chewed
a piece of chalk.
I get bored when
the family talk.
Then someone takes me
for a...**wheelbarrow**?

My Teachers

My teacher's name is Mrs. Large.
She's helped by Mrs. Small.

Miss. Thin comes in
    and she puts up
our paintings
    on the wall.

Big Mr. Bigg's
    the music man.
He's round
    and very tall.

There are
    so **many** teachers,
and I really like
    them all.

Yellow Boots

We're wearing yellow boots
    and the rain has stopped a-thumping.
We're wearing yellow boots
    and now we're puddle jumping!

We're wearing yellow boots
    and the thunder's stopped a-crashing.
We're wearing yellow boots
    and now we're puddle splashing!

Dressing Up

Ben can be a pirate,
and Jade can be a clown.
Jake can be a mailman
walking 'round the town.

Nina can be a princess,
and Mitch can be a knight.
Jess can be a monster
and give us all a **fright**!

Ahmed can be a spaceman,
and Sarah can be a queen.
Jack can be a giant
dressed in red and green.

Jasmine can be a cowgirl,
and Mark can be a king.
Tim can be a wizard
with a magic ring.

Matt can be a doctor,
and Meg can be a nurse.
I will be a teacher
reading out this verse.

Guess Who?

My vest is blue,
    my socks are red.
        A purple hat
            sits on my head.

My shorts are pink,
    my shirt is black.
        Six silver stars
            shine on my back.

My gloves are gold,
    my shoes are brown.
    Who am I?

A circus clown!

99

I'm a Rabbit

I'm a rabbit,
    rolled in a ball.

I'm a horse,
    jumping a wall.

I'm a mouse,
    nibbling at cheese.

I'm a dog,
    scratching its fleas.

I'm a hen,
    pecking at straw.

And I'm a cat,
    asleep on the floor.

The Autumn Leaves

In the autumn
the trees wave in the wind
and the leaves come
tumbling...

down,

down,

down,

down.

Here they come,
hundreds and thousands of leaves
in yellow, red,

hazel,

and

gold,

chocolate brown.

A Week of Winter Weather

On Monday icy rain poured down
and flooded streets all over town.

Monday

Tuesday

Tuesday's gales bashed elm and ash,
dead branches came down with a crash.

On Wednesday bursts of hail and sleet.
No one walked along our street.

Wednesday

Thursday stood out clear and calm,
but the sun was paler than my arm.

Thursday

Friday's frost that bit your ears
was cold enough to freeze your tears.

Friday

Saturday's sky was ghostly gray.
We smashed ice on the lake today.

Saturday

Christmas Eve was Sunday...and
snow fell like foam across the land.

Sunday

Our Snowman

Wow, fatter and fatter and fatter he grows!
We give him button eyes and a red carrot nose.
He has a thick scarf for the North Wind that blows
and slippers to warm his cold toes,

   his cold toes,

      and slippers to warm
      his cold toes!

Up the Wooden Hill

Yawn!
to bed.
wooden hill
up the
going
sleepyhead,
dreamy
I'm a
Ted.
to one-armed
holding on
to bed,
wooden hill
Up the
Yawn!

Counting to Sleep

One. Two. Three. Four.
Five. Six. And Seven more.
Counting spiders,
counting flies,
counting rabbits,
   close
      your
         eyes...

One. Two. Three. Four.
Five. Six. And Seven more.
Counting horses,
counting sheep,
counting seagulls,
   fall...
      asleep.

Wait for Me!

Written and Illustrated
by Eileen Browne

"I'm thirsty and hot,"
said Eddie the elephant.

"Me too," said Piper
the parrot.

"So am I," said
Slippy the snake.

"I've got an idea!" said Molly the monkey.
"Let's go to the cool, sparkly river."

"Hooray!" said everybody.

"But how do we get to the cool, sparkly river?"
asked Eddie the elephant.

"It's easy!" said Piper and Slippy and Molly.
"We cross the wide, sandy desert,
get past the huge pile of rocks,
push through the dark, tangled jungle,
and go over the green, slimy swamp.
That's how we get to the cool, sparkly river."

"Come on, follow us!"

They went to the wide, sandy desert.

"How can we cross it?"
asked Eddie the elephant.

"With a flap of my wings!" said Piper.

"With a slither and a zigzag,"
said Slippy.

"With a hop and
a skip," said Molly.

"Let's go!"

Stomp, stomp, stompety-stomp,
went Eddie the elephant.

"Wait for me!"

They reached the huge pile of rocks.

"How can we get past them?" asked Eddie.

"With a flap and a hop," said Piper.

"With a wiggle and a squeeze,"
said Slippy.

"With a scramble and a climb," said Molly.

Puff-pant, puff-pant, went Eddie.

"Wait for me!"

They came to the dark, tangled jungle.

"How can we get through it?" asked Eddie.

"With a flutter and a flap," said Piper.

"With a weave and a waggle," said Slippy.

"With a swing and a leap," said Molly.

Crash, smash, bumpity-bash, went Eddie.

"Wait for me!"

They got to the green, slimy swamp.

"How can we go over it?" asked Eddie.

"With a flap and a glide," said Piper.

"With a slither and a wriggle," said Slippy.

"With a run and a slide," said Molly.

Squish, squelch, splatter, and splash,
went Eddie.

"Wait for me!"

At last, they arrived at the cool, sparkly river.

"Shall we fly in?" said Piper the parrot.

"Shall we slip in?" said Slippy the snake.

"Shall we climb in?" said Molly the monkey.

121

"Go in how you like...I'm JUMPING," said Eddie.

And Piper and Slippy and Molly all shouted,

"Hey! Wait for me!"

Teddy's Birthday

Written by Anne Faundez
Illustrated by Karen Sapp

The toys are up early. What's happening today?
They bump and they bounce; they're ready to play.

Now they are gathered, it's time for some fun.
It's Teddy's birthday; today he is ONE!

"It's my BIRTHDAY!" cries Teddy,
"I hope everyone's ready!

It's party-time soon,
Let's decorate the room!"

Balloons all around, flowers everywhere,
A banner on the wall, streamers in the air.

"Oh, wow!" says Teddy.
"Party now! Are you ready?"

They share out the hats in blue, green, and red.
Teddy takes TWO to put on his head!

"Let's play some games," say the Twin Yellow Bears.
So they play pass-the-package and musical chairs.

They clap to the music and make lots of noise,
Big Bear, Brown Bear—all of the toys.

Amanda the Panda and Jimmy Giraffe,
Together they dance and soon start to laugh.

Fluffy the Bunny has made lots of treats,
Biscuits and buns, ice cream and sweets.

Everyone's hungry. They each find a seat.
With tummies a-rumbling, they tuck in and eat.

Next, there's a cake on a big silver dish.
Teddy blows hard, and then makes a wish.

The toys clap their hands and together start singing.
Teddy is happy and cannot stop grinning.

"Happy Birthday to you,
Happy Birthday to you!
Happy Birthday, dear Teddy!
Happy Birthday to you!"

There's a gift for Teddy.
He's very excited.
A new bouncy ball!
He's truly delighted!

The toys are now yawning. Such sleepyheads!
They put on pajamas and climb into bed.

After such an exciting and busy, busy day,
They close their eyes
And fall asleep...
right away.

One, Two, Buckle My Shoe

Compiled by Anne Faundez
Illustrated by Brett Hudson

Hickory dickory dock,
The mouse ran up the clock.
The clock struck one,
The mouse ran down,
Hickory dickory dock.

Incy Wincy spider
Climbed up the water spout.
Down came the rain
And washed the spider out.
Out came the sun
And dried up all the rain,
And Incy Wincy spider
Climbed up the spout again.

Higgledy, piggledy, pop!
The dog has eaten
   the mop;
The pig's in a hurry,
The cat's in a flurry,
Higgledy, piggledy, pop!

Oh, the grand old Duke of York,
He had ten thousand men,
He marched them up to the top of the hill,
And he marched them down again.

And when they were up,
  they were up,
And when they were down,
  they were down,
And when they were
  only halfway up,
They were neither up nor down.

If you're happy and you know it,
Clap your hands;
If you're happy and you know it,
Clap your hands;
If you're happy and you know it
And you really want to show it,
If you're happy and you know it,
Clap your hands.

If you're happy and you know it,
Stamp your feet;
If you're happy and you know it,
Stamp your feet;
If you're happy and you know it
And you really want to show it,
If you're happy and you know it,
Stamp your feet.

I'm a little teapot, short and stout,
Here's my handle, here's my spout.
When I see the teacups, hear me shout,
Tip me over and pour me out!

Mary, Mary, quite contrary,
How does your garden grow?
With silver bells and cockleshells,
And pretty maids all in a row.

Hey, diddle, diddle,
The cat and the fiddle,
The cow jumped over
    the moon,
The little dog laughed
To see such sport,
And the dish ran away
    with the spoon.

154

Humpty Dumpty sat on a wall,
Humpty Dumpty had a great fall.
All the king's horses and all the king's men
Couldn't put Humpty together again.

Old MacDonald had a farm,
E-I-E-I-O!

And on that farm he had some pigs,
E-I-E-I-O!

With an oink oink here
and an oink oink there
here an oink
there an oink
everywhere an oink, oink!

Old MacDonald had a farm,
E-I-E-I-O!

And on that farm he had some ducks,
E-I-E-I-O!

With a quack quack here
and a quack quack there
here a quack
there a quack
everywhere a quack,
quack!

Old MacDonald had a farm,
E-I-E-I-O!

I had a little nut tree
And nothing would it bear
But a silver nutmeg and a golden pear.

The King of Spain's daughter came to visit me,
And all for the sake of my little nut tree.

I skipped over water, I danced over sea,
And all the birds in the air couldn't catch me.

The Queen of Hearts
She made some tarts,
All on a summer's day.
The Knave of Hearts
He stole those tarts,
And took them clean away.

Old Mother Hubbard
Went to the cupboard,
To give her poor dog a bone;
But when she got there,
The cupboard was bare
And so the poor dog had none.

She went to the store
To buy him some fruit;
But when she came back,
He was playing the flute.

She went to the hatter's
    To buy him a hat;
But when she came back,
    He was feeding the cat.

The dame made a curtsy,
    The dog made a bow,
The dame said, "Your servant."
    The dog said, "Bow-wow."

161

One, two, buckle my shoe
Three, four, knock at the door
Five, six, pick up sticks
Seven, eight, lay them straight
Nine, ten,
A big fat hen!

Twinkle, twinkle little star,
How I wonder what you are.
Up above the world so high,
Like a diamond in the sky.
Twinkle, twinkle little star,
How I wonder what you are.

Lenny's Lost Spots

Written by Celia Warren
Illustrated by Genny Haines

Lenny was a ladybug.
He was red with black spots.

In the morning, Lenny counted his spots:
One, two, three, four, five, six.

But in the afternoon, Lenny said,
"Where are my spots?
Where have they gone?
This morning I had six
but now I have none."

169

Lenny looked once.
Lenny looked twice.
He thought his spots
were on some dice.
But he was wrong.

Lenny looked down.
Lenny looked up.
He thought his spots
were on a pup.
But he was wrong.

Lenny looked high.
Lenny looked low.

He thought his spots were on a bow.
But he was wrong.

175

Lenny looked here.
Lenny looked there.
He thought his spots
were on a chair.
But he was wrong.

Lenny looked near.
Lenny looked far.
He thought his spots
were on a car.
But he was wrong.

Lenny looked left.
Lenny looked right.
He thought his spots
were on a kite.
But he was wrong.

Lenny went out in the rain.
He said, "My spots are back again."

And he was right.

Little Red Riding Hood

Written by Anne Faundez
Illustrated by Elisa Squillace

Once upon a time, there was a little girl who lived in a village near the woods. Her name was Little Red Riding Hood.

Do you know why she was called Little Red Riding Hood? It was because she had a beautiful red cloak with a hood, specially made by her granny.

The girl was very proud of her cloak and she wore it all the time. So everyone called her Little Red Riding Hood.

One day, Little Red Riding Hood's granny was sick in bed. Little Red Riding Hood helped her mother bake a cake for her granny.

"Little Red Riding Hood, take the cake to your granny. Hurry up, now. Come home before the sun goes down, and don't talk to strangers," said Little Red Riding Hood's mother.

Little Red Riding Hood put the cake in a basket and set off for her granny's cottage, on the other side of the woods.

Granny's House

The sun was high in the sky, and sunlight filled the woods. Birds sang in the trees and little creatures bustled to and fro across the path. Little Red Riding Hood was very happy.

In the distance, Little Red Riding Hood saw a glade full of bright blue and pink flowers. She wandered off the path toward them. Granny will love these flowers, she thought. She picked some flowers and then continued on her way. By this time, the sun was low in the sky.

Suddenly, she heard a noise.
A scuffling, shuffling noise.
A big gray wolf stood in front of her.
  "Where are you going?" he asked.
  "I'm going to visit my granny.
She lives on the other
side of the woods and
she's not very well,"
replied Little Red
Riding Hood.

Little Red Riding Hood
had forgotten that her
mother told her not to
speak to strangers.

"I'd like to visit her, too," said the wolf. "You know what? You go your way and I'll take another path."
The wolf took a short cut.
Little Red Riding Hood continued on her way.

Now and then, Little Red Riding Hood stopped to pick more flowers. By now, the sun had set and the woods were filled with shadows.

The wolf arrived at
Granny's house. He
rapped on the door.
Knock. Knock.
   "Who's there?" asked
Granny.
   "Little Red Riding Hood,"
replied the wolf, in a
squeaky voice.
   "Lift the latch, my dear,
and come in," said Granny.

The wolf bounded into the room.
He yanked the old lady out
of bed and bundled her
into a closet.

He jumped into her bed and
pulled the blankets up to his chin.

Little Red Riding Hood
arrived at her granny's
house. She rapped on
the door.
Knock. Knock.
  "Who's there?" said
a voice.
  "Little Red Riding
Hood," she answered.
  "Lift the latch, my
dear, and come in,"
called the voice.

Now, Little Red Riding Hood had never seen her granny sick in bed. She was surprised.

"Granny, what BIG arms you've got!" she said.

"All the better to hug you with, my dear," said the wolf.

"Granny, what BIG ears you've got!" she said.

"All the better to hear you with, my dear," said the wolf.

"Granny, what BIG eyes you've got!" she said.

"All the better to see you with, my dear," said the wolf.

"Granny, what BIG teeth you've got!" she said.
"All the better to **EAT** you with, my dear!"

And the wolf jumped out of bed and chased
Little Red Riding Hood around the room.

Just at that moment, by the light of the moon, a woodcutter was passing by. He heard a terrible banging and clanging coming from the cottage. He rushed inside and chased that wicked wolf right out of the woods and far away.

Little Red Riding Hood thanked the woodcutter. Then she unpacked her basket, and Granny, the woodcutter, and Little Red Riding Hood sat down to a feast of cake. And they all lived happily ever after.

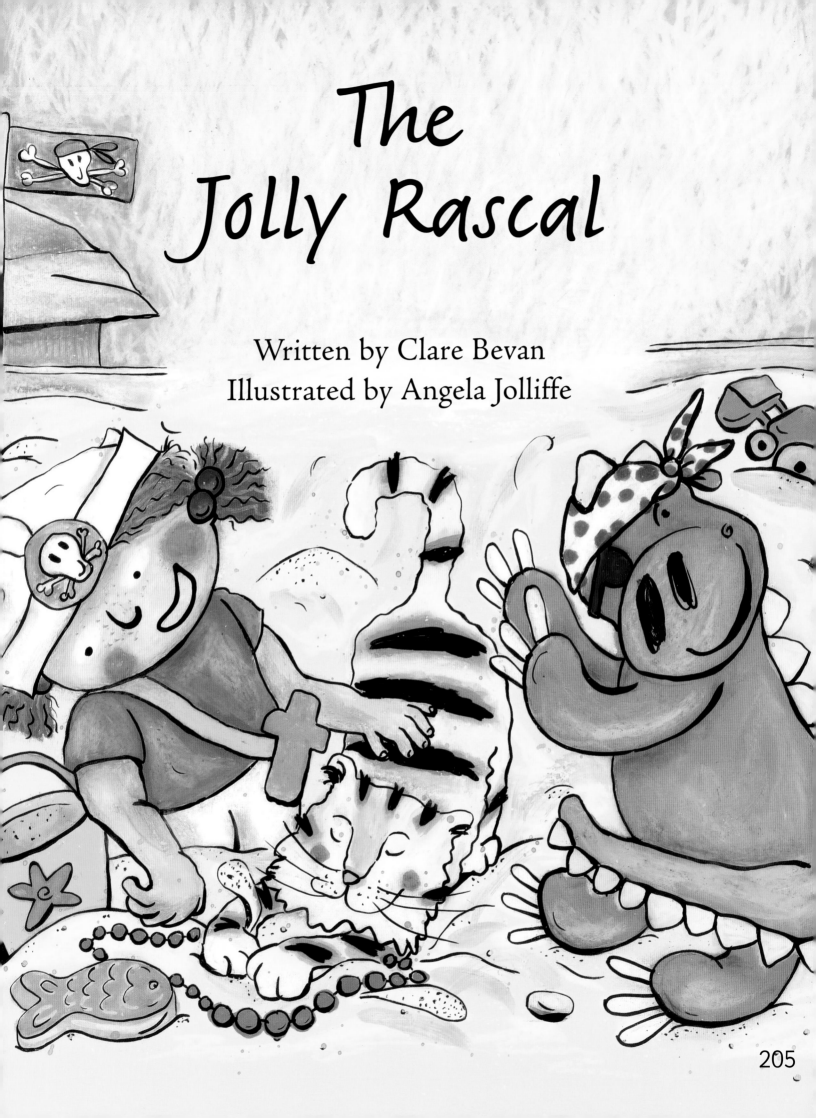

The Jolly Rascal

Written by Clare Bevan

Illustrated by Angela Jolliffe

The Jolly Rascal sails away
Across the stormy sea,
With Captain Flo
And Big Bad Joe,
And pirates, one, two, three.

"Land ho! Land ho!"
 says Captain Flo.
"Let's look for gold," says Joe.
They flap, flap, flap
The treasure map,
The pirates say,
 "Let's go!"

They crawl around the rocky ground,
They crawl around the trees
Where monsters peep,
Where tigers creep,
And pirates rub their knees.

"Away we go," says Captain Flo.
"Away we go," says Joe,
"With me and you,
With Tiger, too,
And pirates in a row."

They find a place where rivers race,
Where fishes swim about,
Where waters CRASH,
And ducks go SPLASH!
The pirates say, "Look out!"

They find a bay where people say,
"We're glad you came this way...
Here's food for you
And Tiger, too."
The pirates shout,
   "Hooray!"

"Follow me,"
    says Captain Flo.
"Follow me," says Joe,
"Past hut and hole
    and totem pole."
The pirates shout,
    "Bravo!"

They stamp their feet to a jungle beat,
They find a magic fountain.
Tiger passes
Stripy grasses
And pirates climb
  a mountain.

215

"Up we go!" says Captain Flo.
"Up we go!" says Joe,
"Climb so high
We touch the sky."
The pirates peer below.

They all look for
a sandy shore,
They all look at the map...
Across the land
They spot the sand!
The pirates cheer and clap.

Says Flo to Joe,
"Sing yo, ho, ho!
The Jolly Rascal Song.
Dig far, dig low,
Dig fast, dig slow!"
The pirates sing along.

They dig the sand with shovels
   and hands,
At last the treasure's here...
The golden rings,
The shiny things!
The pirates clap and cheer.

"Home we go,"
  says Captain Flo.
"Home we go," says Joe,
"With bags of gold
For us to hold."
The pirates sing,
  "Yo, ho!"

The Jolly Rascal sails away
From sand and land and tree,
With Captain Flo
And Big Bad Joe,
And pirates, one, two, three.

So Captain Flo
    and Big Bad Joe,
They cross the sea so deep.
In time for tea,
Then happily...
The pirates
    fall asleep.

Ready for a Picnic

Written by Celia Warren

Illustrated by Elke Zinsmeister

Grandma's Trip

Grandma packed her slippers,
her lipstick, and her comb.
Grandma packed her
   toothbrush
and her bubble-bath foam.

Grandma packed her glasses,
her bikini, and some socks.
Grandma packed her camera
and her jewelry box.

Grandma packed her folding chair,
and all her bags,
then, last of all, before she left,
Grandma packed...Gramps!

Eggs Everywhere

Eggs in England,
Sitting in a cup.
Eggs in America,
Sunny side up.

Ready for a Picnic

One for a sandwich,
Two for a cake,
Three for some ice cream by the lake.

Four for an apple,
Five for a pear,
Six for a picnic—
 see you there!

The Dizzy Hamster

"Tell me, little hamster, how does it feel
going 'round and 'round in your little wheel?"

"Well," said the hamster, "what I have found
is when the wheel stops, then the room goes 'round."

Giraffe

I'd like my head to be
   up in the blue,
Giraffe, giraffe, I'd like to be you.

I'd like to be as tall as a tree,
Giraffe, giraffe, would you
   like to be me?

I like the way you make
   funny faces,
Giraffe, giraffe, would you
   like to change places?

What Can I Be?

I can be a penguin and waddle as I walk,
I can be a parrot with a funny way to talk,
I can be a hamster and curl up small,
I can be a dog and bring you a ball,
I can be a monkey and swing from a tree
But, if it's okay, I can just be me.

Painting

Tommy painted daddy,
Tommy painted mommy,
but they both got very cross
when Tommy painted Tommy.

Off We Go

Up the hill

By the waterfall, then...

Over the wall,

Tumbling, turning

Down the road,

All
the
way
down

Hats

Paper hats for parties,
Flowered hats for show,
Sun hats in summer,
Everywhere you go.

Hard hats for bricklayers,
A white hat for a cook,
Stocking caps in winter,
Everywhere you look.

Riddles

The shape
of a plate or a
coin, the full moon
or a bowl of soup, the
shape of a button, the
sun or a wheel, what
shape is as round
as a hoop?

A
roof
or the shape
of the ear of a cat;
three sides and three
corners, what shape is that?

Landscape

My potato is an island.
The gravy is the sea.
The peas are people swimming.
The biggest one is me.

My carrots are whales
That make the sea wavy
But the big, brown blobs
Are LUMPS in the gravy!

Washing the Dishes

Knives and forks and spoons in a jumble,
Dishes clatter, splash, and tumble,
Bubbles in the sink where fingers fumble,
 Doing the dishes.
  SPLASH!

Ten Bold Pirates

Ten bold pirates,
    all shipshape,
Two got seasick
    and that left eight.

Eight bold pirates
    playing tricks,
Two met a shark
    and that left six.
Six bold pirates,
    tired of being poor,
Two found treasure
    and that left four.

Four bold pirates
    feeling blue,
Two swam home again
    and that left two.

Two bold pirates
    drinking rum,
They fell asleep
    and that left none.

Song Birds

Song birds up the holly,
Song birds up the oak.
One bird singing on the chimney,
A song bird in the smoke.

Daffodil Dip

Dip, dip, daffodil,
Sing and shout.
Dip, dip, daffodil,
You are OUT.

Dip, dip, daisy,
Where we sit,
Dip, dip, daisy,
You are IT.

This Little Poem

This little poem,
You can keep in your hands.
Sometimes it wiggles,
And sometimes it stands.

It likes to wave,
It loves to clap,
Then it falls asleep,
Face down in your lap.

The Wonderful Gift

Written by Clare Bevan
Illustrated by Kelly Waldek

When the little princess was born, the King and Queen were VERY excited.

"She will have EVERYTHING she wants," said the King.

"She will be the happiest princess in the whole world," said the Queen.

They gave her a golden rattle and a teddy bear with soft, silky fur. They rocked her in a silver cradle.

The little princess cried and cried and CRIED.

246

"Give the little princess a beautiful name," said the Wise Man. "Then she will be happy."
So the King and the Queen looked through a big book and chose the most beautiful name they could find.

"She will be called Princess Starlight," said the Queen.
"Her room will be decorated with stars," said the King.

Princess Starlight cried and cried and CRIED.

One year later, Princess Starlight was STILL crying.
"Give her a birthday party," said the Wise Man.
"Everyone will bring her a present.
Then she will be happy."

So the King wrote letters on shiny paper to all the Fairy Godmothers. The Queen gave Princess Starlight a blue party dress, scattered with stars.

Princess Starlight cried and cried and CRIED.

It was a very nice party. There was a big
birthday cake with one candle and hundreds
of sugar stars. There were balloons shaped
like stars, and a mountain of presents
wrapped in starry paper.

"Now our little princess will be happy," said the King.
  "Now she will smile," said the Queen.

Princess Starlight looked at her cake and her balloons and her presents. She was quiet for a whole minute.

Then she started to CRY.

The Fairy Godmothers said, "We will give our presents to Princess Starlight. Then she will be happy."

They gave her a tiny flying horse, a talking mirror that could tell jokes, a crown made of moonbeams, and a box of magic jewels.

Princess Starlight looked at
her presents for a long time.
Everyone held their breath.
Then she CRIED.

Many years went by.

Princess Starlight still wore beautiful dresses
scattered with stars. Inside her starry room,
she kept her magical presents.

Every day, jesters
and jugglers tried
to make her smile.

Every day, the King
and Queen tried to
make her happy.

But she STILL
felt sad and
wanted to cry.

One day, she heard someone singing outside her window. "Who is THAT?" she asked grumpily.

Princess Starlight stomped down the palace stairs to see the King and Queen. "Someone is making an AWFUL noise outside my window," she complained. "You must stop him right now."

"Of course," said the King and Queen. "If it will make you happy."

So the palace policeman found the singer and marched him indoors.

It was the gardener's son.
He looked very grubby,
but he had twinkly eyes.

"Why are you so happy?"
asked Princess Starlight angrily.

The gardener's son smiled. "Because the sun is shining and the flowers are growing," he answered.

"I don't understand," said Princess Starlight with a frown. "I have all my treasures, yet I feel sad."

"That is because you do not have the Wonderful Gift of Happiness," said the gardener's son.

"Where can we find this Wonderful Gift?" asked the King and Queen.

"Princess Starlight must find it for herself," said the gardener's son.

He led Princess Starlight outside and showed her how to dig in the dirt. Together, they planted seeds and sang funny songs. They worked for many weeks.

One day, Princess Starlight ran indoors. She was grubby, but she was smiling and her arms were full of starry flowers.

"I still haven't found the Gift of Happiness," she laughed.

But, of course, she had. Hadn't she?

Katie's Mom is a Mermaid

Written by Hannah Ray
Illustrated by Dawn Vince

There's a new girl in my class,
Her name is Katie Lou,
Her hair is shiny, all golden curls,
Her eyes are sparkly blue.

Best friends with new girl Katie,
Is what I'd like to be,
But her life sounds so fantastic,
Would she be friends with me?

She says her mom's a mermaid,
Who sings in an ocean band.
An octopus plays the drums,
You can hear him on dry land.

Her dad's a famous cowboy,
Who rides a big white horse.
He gallops through the wild, wild west,
Catching outlaws, of course!

Katie's granny is a pilot,
Wearing goggles and a scarf.
She loops the loop and wiggles her wings,
To make the people laugh.

Her brother is a strongman,
Although he's only three,
Lifting elephants on one hand,
For all the world to see.

Katie's house is a castle,
With a drawbridge and a moat,
She says it gets quite chilly,
So she wears a giant coat.

There are butlers and a gardener,
A driver and a cook,
So grand it is, that Katie says,
A queen came to take a look.

Last Friday Katie asked me,
To go around and play.
But after saying that I would,
She was quiet all day.

Katie led the way back home,
We wandered down the street.
I asked her where the castle was,
But she looked at her feet.

And when we got to Katie's house,
What a big shock I had!
A house like mine, with a bright red door,
Opened by Katie's dad.

A regular guy, not a cowboy,
Her dad delivers mail.
And Katie's mom, I soon found out,
Has legs and not a tail.

Katie's brother played with toys,
He showed me his best bear.
And her granny was just like mine,
Though she did have bright pink hair!

But Katie still looked worried,
"I'm very sorry," she said.
She looked like she might start to cry,
Her face was very red.

Katie said, in a tiny voice,
"I told a fib or two,
But I wanted you to like me,
It's hard being brand new!"

But I am just like Katie,
I love to play pretend,
And now we are two princesses,
And are the best of friends!

Tiddalik the Frog

Written by Anne Faundez

Illustrated by Sanja Rescek

Long ago, in the Dreamtime, a huge red frog roamed the earth. His name was Tiddalik.

Tiddalik was so large that his back touched the sky. He was so wide that he filled the space between two mountain ranges. When he moved, the ground trembled and his feet made holes as big as valleys.

One day, he woke up from a very bad sleep.
He was VERY, VERY grumpy!
He was also VERY, VERY thirsty!

"Water! Water!" he bellowed.
His words made the clouds crackle with thunder.

He found a river and drank up all the water.
He found a lake and emptied that, too.
He kept on drinking until every waterhole was dry.

Tiddalik was now bulging with
water and ready to burst.

He was too uncomfortable
to move. He shut his
eyes and fell into a
long, deep sleep.

The days went by.

Tiddalik slept.

There was no sign
of rain in the skies.

The sun scorched
the earth. The
grasses withered
and the trees lost
their leaves.

The beautiful green
earth became hard
and cracked.

Kangaroo, Kookaburra, and Platypus
were anxious. They had watched
Tiddalik drinking up all the water.
Now their land was turning to dust.

"The earth is so cracked that I can't hop around anymore," grumbled Kangaroo.

"There's nowhere for me to swim," moaned Platypus.

"Tiddalik MUST return our water!" said Kookaburra.

But the animals were scared to talk to Tiddalik. He was still so grumpy!

"I know," said Kookaburra.
"Let's make him laugh. Then
he'll spill out the water."

So Kookaburra flew right up to
Tiddalik. She sang some funny
songs. She wiggled and jiggled
and danced around.

Tiddalik opened one eye.
He shut it again.

Platypus went up to Tiddalik. She told a
few jokes and then she flipped and flopped
and shuffled around.

Tiddalik opened the other eye.
He shut it again.

Next, it was Kangaroo's turn.
He loved to show off.
He twirled and whirled,
and thumped and
bumped his tail around.

Tiddalik opened both eyes.
He shut them again.
He was still bored.

Just then, Little Eel came rushing towards the animals.

"Let me make Tiddalik laugh!"
he cried.

He raced towards
Tiddalik, turning
somersaults all
the way.

Little Eel landed on Tiddalik's bulging stomach.
He scrambled to get himself upright.
He teetered and tottered and then stood,
looking up at the gigantic frog.

Tiddalik opened his eyes. He was
so astonished to see Little Eel,
all shivering and shaking,
sitting right on his belly.

Tiddalik made a rumbling noise.
He chuckled—and a trickle of water
dribbled from his mouth.

He chuckled some more.

Soon, he was rumbling with laughter.
Water spilled from his mouth and ran down his sides.
Tiddalik couldn't stop laughing at the sight of
Little Eel sitting on his belly.
As he laughed, he felt less grumpy.

Soon, the land was awash with water.
The grasses began to grow again, and tiny leaves
began to cover the bare branches of the trees.

And do you know what? To this day, Tiddalik
has never again emptied the land of water.
Why?

Well, Little Eel knows just what to do now
when Tiddalik gets grumpy...and thirsty!

Index

Index of first lines of poetry and nursery rhymes